D1102561

90710 000 434 048

WEB WORLD

Steve Barlow and Steve Skidmore

Illustrated by Santy Gutiérrez

LONDON·SYDNEY

Franklin Watts
First published in Great Britain in 2019 by The Watts Publishing Group

Credits
Series Editor: Adrian Cole
Project Editor: Katie Woolley
Consultant: Jackie Hamley
Designer: Cathryn Gilbert
Illustrations: Santy Gutiérrez

HB ISBN 978 1 4451 5979 9
PB ISBN 978 1 4451 5980 5
Library ebook ISBN 978 1 4451 5981 2

Printed in China.

Franklin Watts
An imprint of
Hachette Children's Group
Part of The Watts Publishing Group
Carmelite House
50 Victoria Embankment
London EC4Y 0DZ

An Hachette UK Company
www.hachette.co.uk

www.franklinwatts.co.uk

THE BADDIES

Lord and Lady Evil	Dr Y

They want to rule the galaxy.

THE GOODIES

Boo Hoo   Jet   Tip

They want to stop them.

7

8

"I can't believe that you are scared
of spiders," said Jet.
"Believe it. I am!" said Tip.
Jet shook her head. "Spiders can't do
you any harm..."

The call continued, "We have crashed on Planet Arakno. We need your help! Please rescue us!"

"Let's go!" said Jet

15

"What is the matter?" asked Jet.

"I spy a spider!" said Tip.

"Not again!" laughed Jet. "Are you scared of a little spider?"

"No! I am scared of a great big one! And its friends!"

18

" 'Spiders can't do you any harm!' Ha!"
said Tip.

"Can't you put a more positive spin on
this?" said Jet.

"We are going to die!" said Tip. "What
is there to be positive about!"

"I have contacted Boo Hoo 2. She is my sister," said Boo Hoo.

"You have a sister?" asked Jet.

"We have the same motherboard," replied Boo Hoo. "She is bringing a vacuum cleaner."

"What good will that do?" cried Tip.

"Wait and see," said Boo Hoo. "Take my hands."

Before the spiders can attack.